Stories of MONSTERS

Russell Punter

Illustrated by
Mike Phillips

Reading Consultant: Alison Kelly
Roehampton University

Contents

Chapter 1

The bed monster's secret

Gggrhh

Ben Boggle lay awake in a cold sweat. How could he sleep with a monster under his bed?

Every evening it was the same story. As soon as Ben switched off his bedside light, the monster woke with a snort.

Grrrgggh
Gruggluggle

All through the night, the creature gurgled and growled in the shadows.

Ben had never dared to look under his bed. He was too terrified of what he might see.

Perhaps the monster had ten eyes...

or long, slimy tentacles...

or huge, sharp teeth...

...or all of these!

At school, Ben could hardly keep his eyes open.

"That's the third time this week you've fallen asleep in class," yelled his teacher. Mr. Grizzle liked people to be awake in his mathematics lessons.

Even when he was wide awake, Ben was hopeless with numbers. They were even more difficult when he felt sleepy.

Get to bed earlier, young man!

Unless Ben could get rid of the monster, Mr. Grizzle would be shouting at him every day.

Tired and worried, Ben was walking home when he spotted something in a shop window.

"Maybe that book has something about bed monsters," Ben thought. He dashed inside.

As soon as he got home, Ben read the book from cover to cover. But there was no mention of monsters under the bed.

Chapter XII

What monsters eat

Monsters like to eat:
- little kids
- monster hunters
- small furry animals
- big furry animals
- chocolate chip cookies

"What a waste of money," thought Ben. Then he had an idea. Perhaps the book could help him after all...

Ben decided to build a monster trap. He raided the chocolate chip cookie jar and took a net from his dad's fishing box. In no time at all, his trap was ready.

That night, he climbed into bed, switched off the light and waited.

At first, Ben's room was spookily silent. Then he heard a crunching, munching sound followed by a whoosh. His monster trap had worked!

Nervously, Ben crept over to the net. But nothing could have prepared him for what happened next...

"Please don't hurt me," squeaked a tiny voice. The smallest monster in the world was tangled in the net.

"I can't believe I was scared of you," cried Ben.

"I know," the monster said sadly. "I'm too small to scare anyone. That's why I hid under your bed. I didn't want you to see me."

"I'm the most useless monster alive," she wailed and started to sob. Ben began to feel sorry for the strange little creature.

The monster sniffed.

"It's impossible to scare people when you only weigh fifteen ounces," she said. "I mean, that's less than half a kilo."

"Is it really?" said Ben.

"Oh yes," replied the monster. "I may be small, but I'm not stupid."

This gave Ben such a great idea that he grinned all night, even in his sleep.

He was still grinning the next day at school as Mr. Grizzle began the lesson.

"Ben Boggle," barked Mr. Grizzle. "What is nine times eight?"

"Seventy two," said Ben confidently.

Mr. Grizzle couldn't believe his ears. "Oh, that's correct," he said, shakily. He asked Ben problem after problem. Ben answered every one correctly.

Mr. Grizzle was amazed. "Well done, Ben," he said. "What an astonishing improvement!"

Luckily, no one but Ben had heard the tiny voice whispering the answers.

Ben smiled to himself. Mathematics is a lot easier when you have a monster in your pocket.

Chapter 2

Return of the ice monster

Frankie Frost was fed up. All her friends had gone to the mountains to ski and she had to stay behind and help her mother.

Frankie gazed sadly out of the window.

"The gang will be drinking hot chocolate in the log cabin, about now," she thought. Bernie her dog looked as sad as she did.

You were looking forward to it too, weren't you boy?

Frankie sighed and swept up another pile of frizzy hair.

Just then, one of Frankie's friends rushed in. The look of terror on his face made the customers spill their coffee.

"What's the matter, Chip?" asked Frankie. "Where are the others?"

"The ice m...m...monster got them," he stuttered.

20

"What a lot of nonsense, Chip Redwood," said Mrs. Frost. "*Ice monster*, indeed."

"They're in trouble," insisted Chip. "I'm getting my dad."

"And I'm going to look for my friends," said Frankie, snatching her coat.

Frankie raced out before anyone could stop her.

Come on, Bernie!

Soon, she and her faithful little dog were crunching through the snow up the mountain.

Frankie stared at the frozen mountainside. Her friends were nowhere to be seen.

Then she noticed a huge crater in the snow. Next to it was another, and another...

They look like...

...footprints!

CRUNCH
CRUNCH

They were ice monster footprints. Frankie's heart thumped as she ran for cover.

Come here, Bernie!

24

But Bernie was braver than he looked. He was determined to tackle the monster.

Grrr! Woof! Woof!

Unhappily for Bernie, the ice monster was in a very bad mood. He took one look at Bernie and let out an icy roar.

As Frankie watched
helplessly, Bernie was frozen
to the spot by the monster's
chilling breath.

26

The monster picked up the little dog like a lollipop and stomped on his way.

Frankie followed the massive creature across the mountain. "I've got to rescue poor Bernie," she thought.

27

It wasn't long before the
monster reached a sparkling
cave of ice.

Frankie wasn't sure if her
teeth were chattering with
cold or fear. She crept inside
and stared in horror.

There, glistening in the corner, stood her friends — frozen like icicles.

"You can join the rest of my lunch," growled the monster, sticking Bernie in the ground.

Unless Frankie acted quickly, her friends would be eaten alive.

As she sneaked outside to find help, Frankie noticed smoke rising from the gang's log cabin. She rushed over. The smoke had given her an idea.

The monster was just about
to take his first bite of lunch,
when a sweet, chocolatey
smell wafted into the cave.

Mmm!
Something
smells good.

He didn't know what it was,
but it certainly smelled better
than the little hairy creature
he'd found outside.

The monster followed the smell to the cabin and crashed through the wall.

He'd never eaten anything that wasn't ice-cold. But that didn't stop him from gulping down the steaming, chocolate drink.

In between gulps, the
monster spotted
Frankie.

Ah, something
chewy!

The creature tried to chase
her, but his legs wouldn't
move.

"Aagh!" he cried. There was
a puddle where his legs used to
be. He was melting.

33

The monster gave one last desperate roar, but it was too late.

Frankie watched as the monster dripped and drizzled. Soon, there was nothing left of him but a pool of slushy water.

At that moment, Chip and his dad appeared.

"Where is everyone, Frankie?" asked Mr. Redwood.

"They're in the cave," she cried. "This way!"

The three of them loaded Bernie and the frozen children onto Mr. Redwood's truck and they drove back to town.

Back home, Frankie grabbed
every hairdryer she could find.
"Set them to super warm!"
she told the others, and they
blasted her frozen friends with
hot air.

As soon as everyone was
back to normal, Chip's dad
took them all out for burgers
and colas – without ice!

Chapter 3

Attack of the swamp monster

Tom Smudge loved to listen to his Grandpa Jess tell creepy stories about the old days.

"Did I ever tell you about the swamp monster?" asked the old man one afternoon.

"No," gulped Tom nervously.

"It happened years ago," began Grandpa Jess. "I was a farmhand on Roy's ranch, when one of the cows went missing."

"I searched all day with no luck. As night fell, I spotted a muddy trail leading to the middle of the swamp..."

"What happened next?" asked Tom, with a shiver.

"A terrible, slithering sound filled the air, and I found myself face to face with a horrible, hideous..."

Tom, stop bothering your grandpa!

Mrs. Smudge suddenly burst into the room waving a piece of paper at Tom.

"I need you to go to the store and get these things!" she said.

"Can't I hear the end of Grandpa's story first?" begged Tom.

Grocery list
Soap for Grandpa
2 large bottles of bubble bath
Lots of broccoli
Small cabbage
Peas

"No. Now, off you go," said Mrs. Smudge. "And hurry back," she added. "You haven't had a bath yet."

Tom groaned. He hated baths.

He was trudging back from the store when his friends asked him to play football. Thinking of the waiting bath, Tom quickly agreed.

By the time the game ended, it was almost dark. Tom decided to take a shortcut home across the swamp.

He'd only been walking for a minute, when he heard a sinister, squelching sound. Green stalks seemed to be curling around him.

These weeds are very thick.

But they weren't weeds that Tom could feel tightening around his ankles...

Tom struggled in the slimy
creature's grasp. The more he
squirmed, the tighter the
monster squeezed.

Tom wished he'd never stopped to play football.

The monster dragged him closer to its huge, slimy, smelly mouth.

Suddenly there was a crack. The monster had smashed the bottles in Tom's bag.

In seconds, the murky swamp water became a mass of sweet-smelling bubbles.

The monster choked and spluttered on the foamy water. Tom slipped from its grasp. They were both getting the bath of their lives.

By now, several people had heard Tom's shouts and come to help. They took one look at the new, squeaky-clean monster and burst out laughing.

The monster was so embarrassed, it swam off and was never seen again.

As for Tom, he had the best reward ever. He didn't need a bath for a week.

There are lots more great stories for you to read:

Usborne Young Reading: Series One
Aladdin and his Magical Lamp
Ali Baba and the Forty Thieves
Animal Legends
Stories of Dragons
Stories of Giants
Stories of Gnomes & Goblins
Stories of Magical Animals
Stories of Pirates
Stories of Princes & Princesses
Stories of Witches
The Burglar's Breakfast
The Dinosaurs Next Door
The Monster Gang
Wizards

Usborne Young Reading: Series Two
A Christmas Carol
Aesop's Fables
Gulliver's Travels
Jason & The Golden Fleece
Robinson Crusoe
The Adventures of King Arthur
The Amazing Adventures of Hercules
The Amazing Adventures of Ulysses
The Clumsy Crocodile
The Fairground Ghost
The Incredible Present
The Story of Castles
The Story of Flying
The Story of Ships
The Story of Trains
Treasure Island

Series editor:
Lesley Sims

This edition first published in 2007 by Usborne Publishing Ltd.,
Usborne House, 83-85 Saffron Hill, London EC1N 8RT, England.
www.usborne.com
Copyright © 2007, 2004 Usborne Publishing Ltd.